P9-CQP-698

D0014894

# TIME FLIES

IOWA CITY
FEB

DISCARDED
from Iowa City Public Library

ERIC ROHMANN

Crown Publishers *New York*

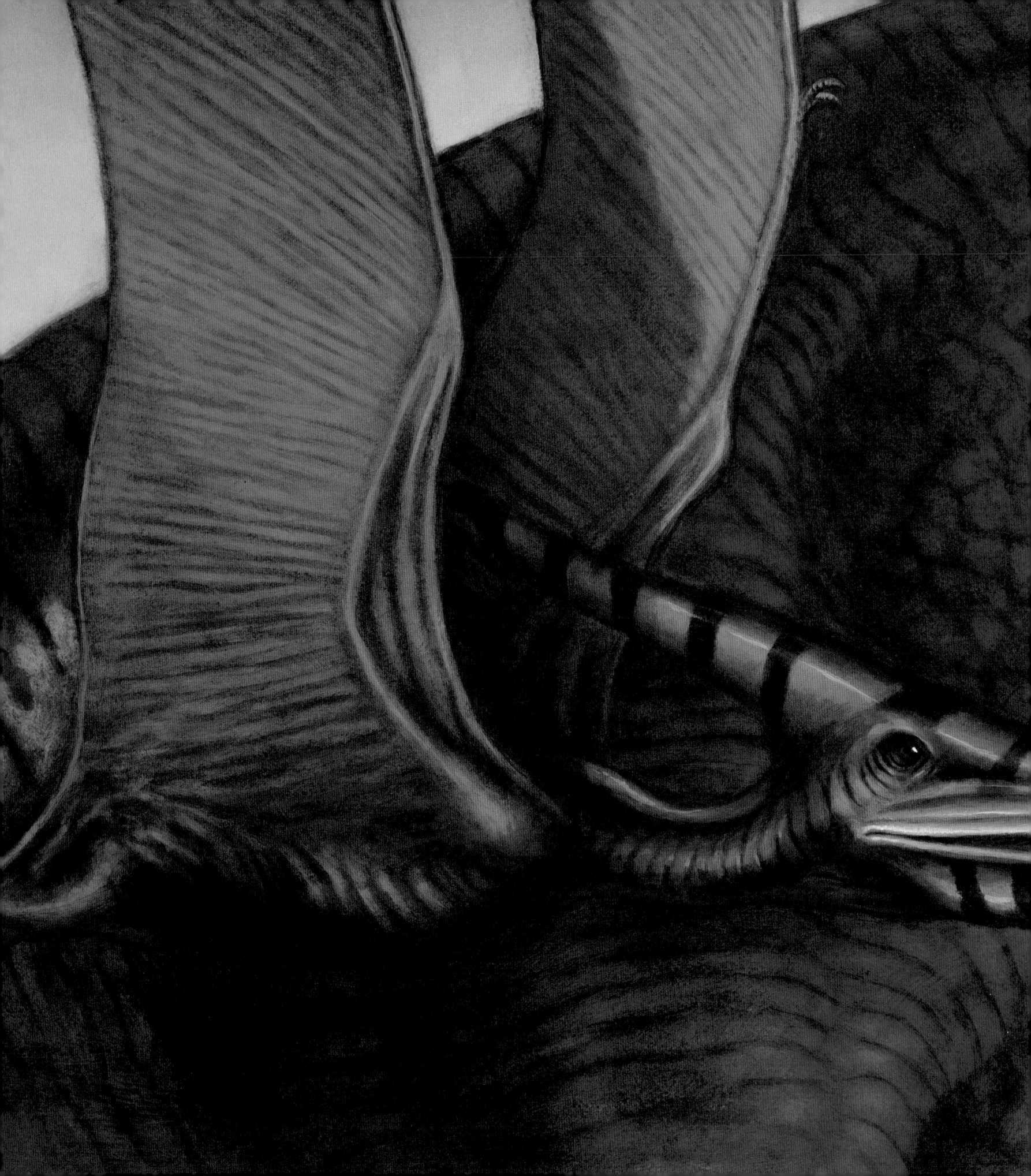

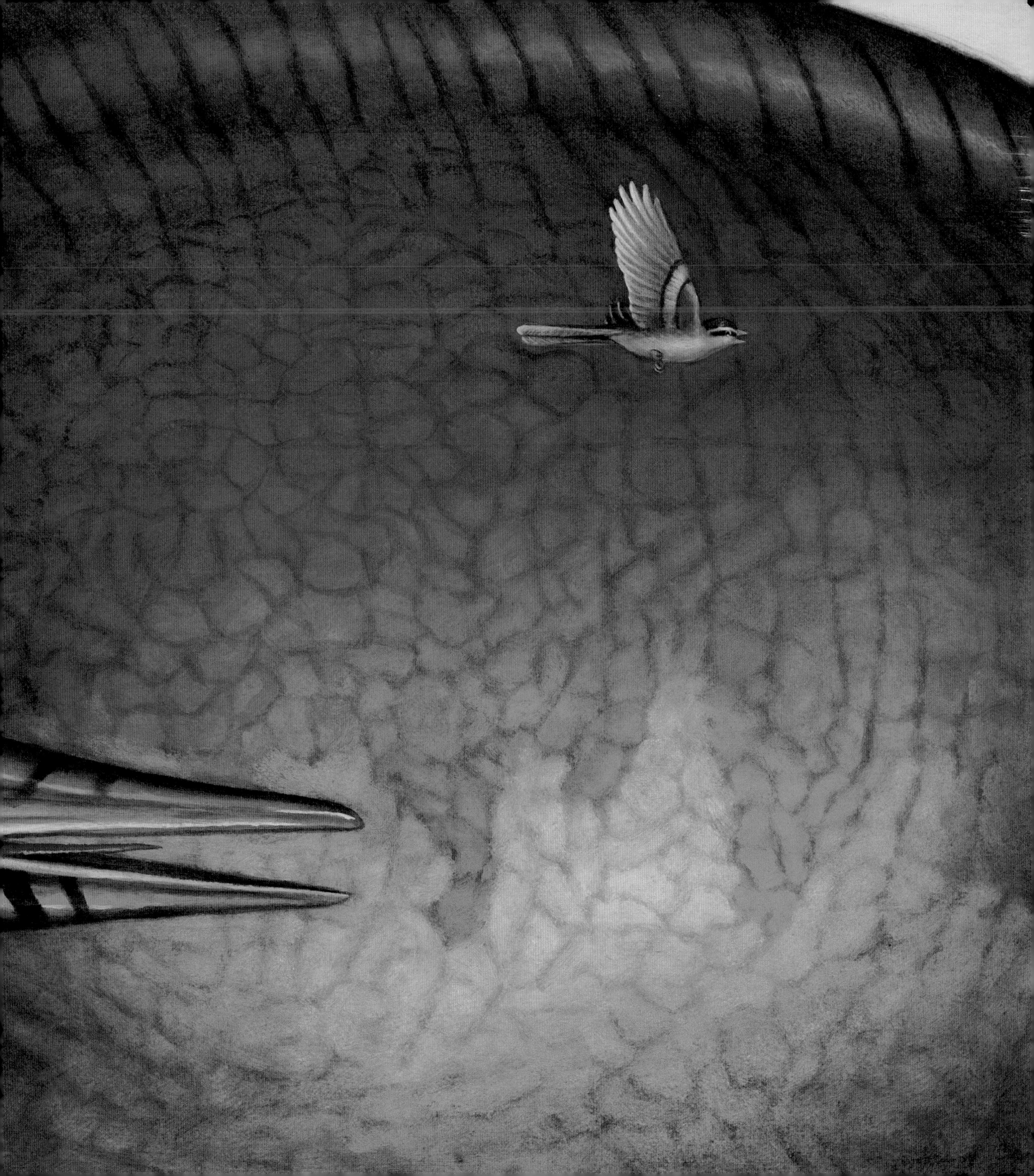

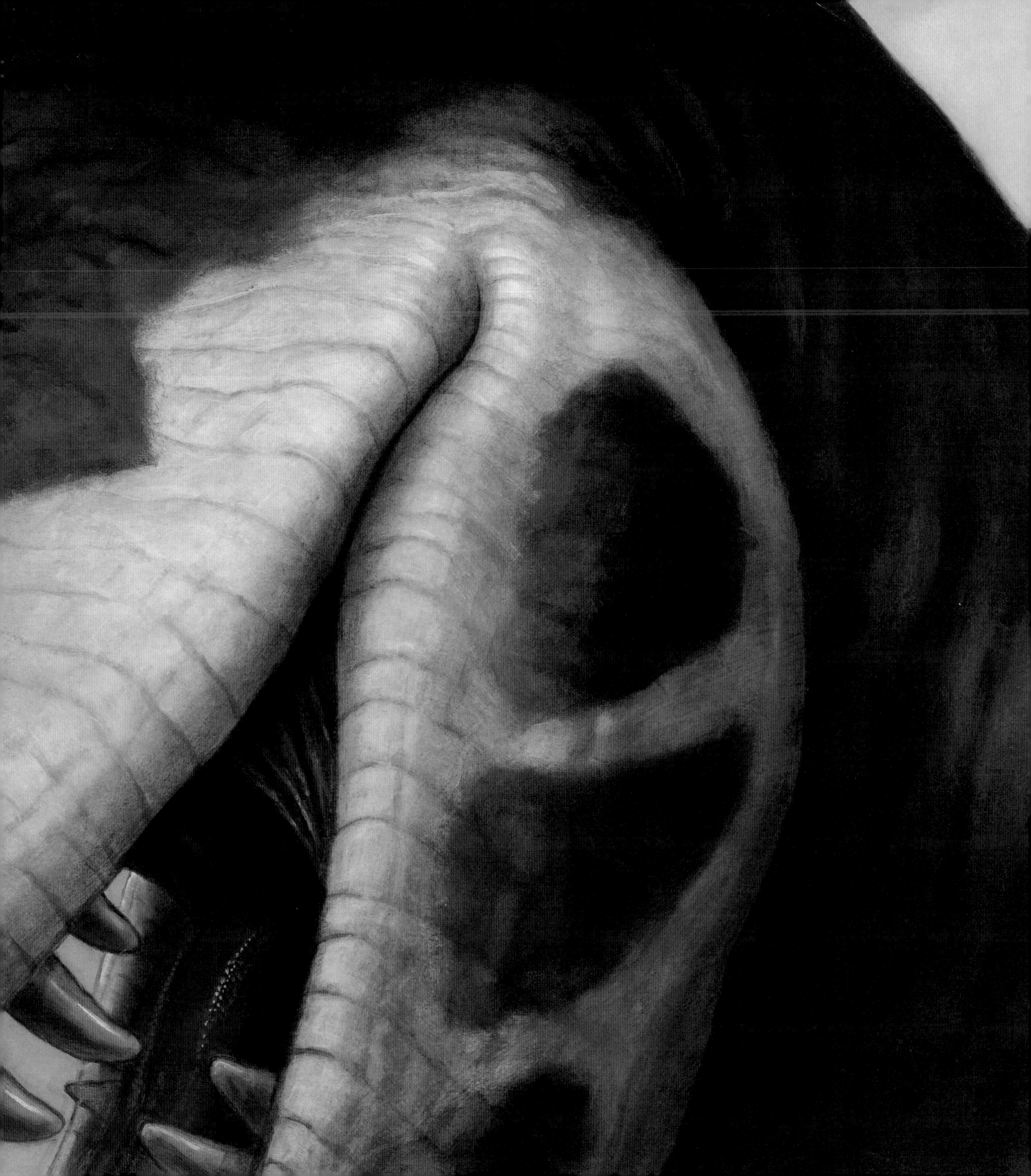

Copyright © 1994 by Eric Rohmann

All rights reserved. No part of this book may be reproduced or transmitted in any form or by any means, electronic or mechanical, including photocopying, recording, or by any information storage and retrieval system, without permission in writing from the publisher. Published by Crown Publishers, an imprint of Random House Children's Books, a division of Random House, Inc., New York.

CROWN and colophon are trademarks of Random House, Inc.

www.randomhouse.com/kids

*Library of Congress Cataloging-in-Publication Data*

Rohmann, Eric.

Time flies / by Eric Rohmann.

p. cm.

SUMMARY: A wordless tale in which a bird flying around the dinosaur exhibit of a natural history museum has an unsettling experience when the dinosaur seems to come to life and view the bird as a potential meal.

ISBN: 0-517-59598-2 (trade) — 0-517-59599-0 (lib. bdg.)

[1. Stories without words. 2. Birds—Fiction. 3. Dinosaurs—Fiction. 4. Museums—Fiction.] I. Title.

PZ7.R6413Ti 1994

[E]—dc20 93-28200

MANUFACTURED IN CHINA July 2003 11 10 9